# HAROLD'S
# TREASURE HUNT

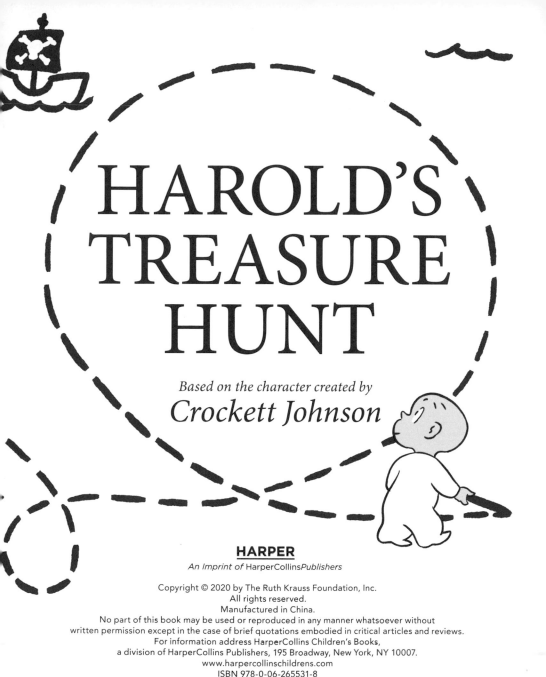

# HAROLD'S TREASURE HUNT

*Based on the character created by*
## Crockett Johnson

### HARPER
*An Imprint of HarperCollinsPublishers*

Copyright © 2020 by The Ruth Krauss Foundation, Inc.
All rights reserved.
Manufactured in China.
For information address HarperCollins Children's Books,
a division of HarperCollins Publishers, 195 Broadway, New York, NY 10007.
www.harpercollinschildrens.com
ISBN 978-0-06-265531-8
20 21 22 23 24   SCP   10 9 8 7 6 5 4 3 2 1   ❖ First Edition

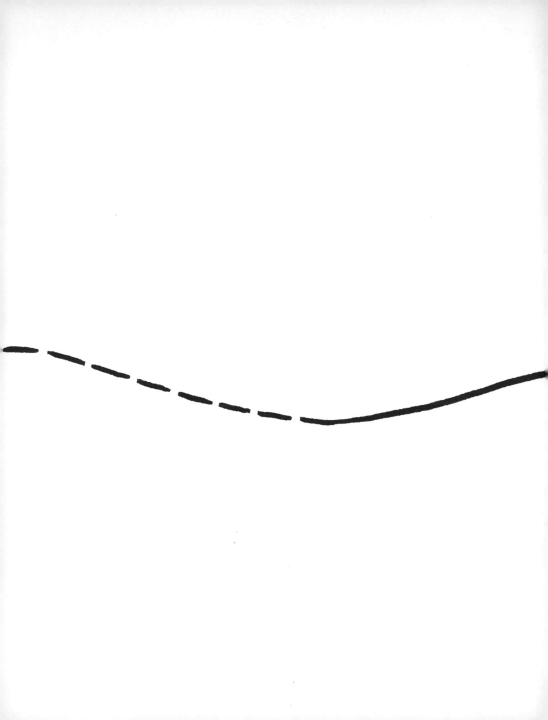

One clear night, Harold got up and went for a walk on the beach. He took his purple crayon and asked the moon to come and light the way.

The beach was empty and peaceful once the families went home.

The salty smell of the ocean reminded
Harold of tales of pirates and adventure
on the high seas.

He decided to find some pirates and join
their adventure.

Harold knew that the best place to find pirates
was on a pirate ship.

He found an anchor with a big chain.

It went up and up and up.

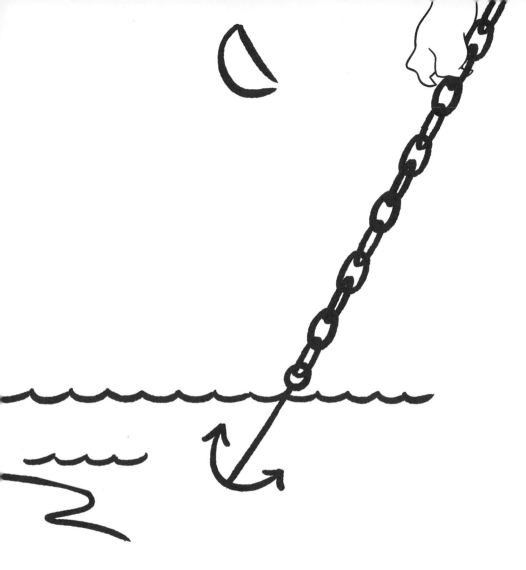

Harold was sure a ship must be attached to
the other end. So up he climbed.

He put a porthole at the top of the chain so he
could climb aboard.

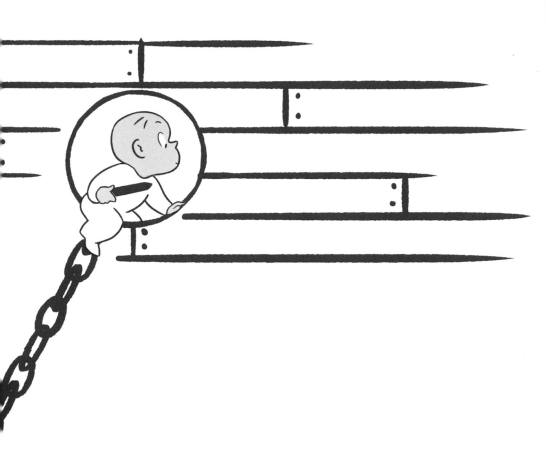

There might be treasure, Harold thought, as he climbed in.

Harold hoped the pirates would be asleep since it was nighttime.

He knew pirates could be grumpy if you wake them up, so he stayed very quiet so as not to disturb them.

Harold checked and made sure

that everything was shipshape.

He wondered what it would be like to be a pirate.

He made a pirate hat and used his purple
crayon like a sword. He jumped around,
pretending to be a pirate, until . . .

. . . a pirate came along. He was indeed grumpy,
so Harold gave him his hat back.

Harold asked the grumpy pirate about
treasure. He didn't seem to want to talk
about that.

The grumpy pirate waved his sword. Harold wondered what the pirate might be trying to tell him. Eventually Harold got the point.

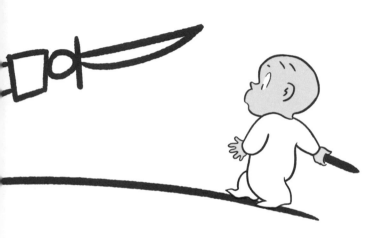

The grumpy pirate wanted him to walk the
plank. Now Harold knew that the pirate life
was not the life for him.

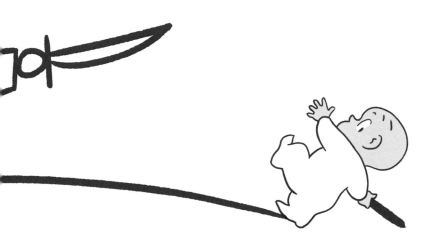

Harold inched backward but lost his balance.
As he began to fall, he wondered if the water
below would be cold.

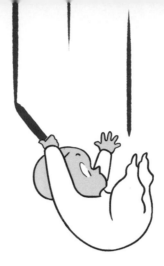

Harold fell down, down, down through the air,
holding his crayon tightly.

Harold held his breath . . .

. . . as he dove underwater.

Harold wondered if there was treasure to
find under the sea. He swam deeper to find
someone who might know.

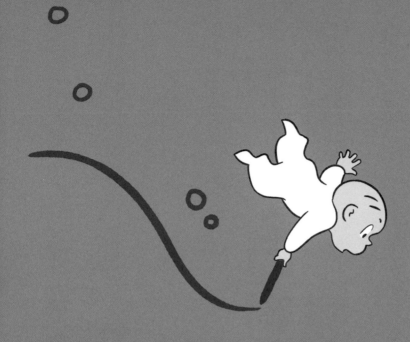

It was hard to see under the sea, but he spotted

something nearby. Was it treasure?

Harold had a strange feeling that he was being watched. Suddenly, an octopus floated by.

With eight arms, an octopus could surely point
him in the right direction, Harold thought.

Unfortunately, they didn't see eye to eye. So
Harold swam on, looking for someone else who
might know. He came upon a smart little fish.

And then another and another, until Harold

was swimming with a whole school of fish.

He asked if they had learned of any sunken
treasure.

They didn't seem to understand.

No matter, Harold thought.

He was happy to have some company.

But they were moving very quickly.

Harold wondered why they were in such a rush.

Suddenly another fish came into view.

It was much bigger than the other fish.

Harold wondered if this was their teacher.

Then he realized what sort of fish this was.

It was a shark with lots of sharp teeth.

Harold clutched his purple crayon and swam
away as fast as he could.

He swam to the bottom and quickly made a
safe place to hide.

When the coast was clear, Harold set out again.
He was feeling tired from all the swimming, so
he decided to walk.

Then something in the seaweed caught his eye.

It was a mermaid.

The mermaid was part fish and part person.
Harold asked her if she knew where to find
treasure.

But she was busy playing with a starfish, and
he didn't want to interupt them.

So Harold climbed on the back of a giant sea turtle that was swimming by and asked her for a ride.

Harold had heard that sea turtles were fast

swimmers.

They took off at top speed.

The sea turtle brought him to the shore of a
deserted island. Harold felt relieved to be back
on land again.

This was just the kind of place where pirates would hide treasure, Harold thought. So he began to search.

After a while he found a cave.

Harold knew caves were damp and spooky . . .

. . . and might even be filled with bats.

He wished the moon could come in and light the way.

The cave *was* dark, very dark. But Harold
could tell someone had been here before.

He saw a picture of a horse and other animals
on the wall. But there was no sign of treasure.

Harold was getting tired of hunting

for treasure.

He was starting to wish he was home,
when he bumped into something.

Harold thought it might be a treasure chest, but
it was very dark and he couldn't see for sure.

He needed some light. Harold wished he could
see the moon or, even better, the sun. But there
were no windows in a dark cave.

Then Harold remembered his purple crayon.

Harold drew the curtains and the sun shined through big and bright.

And there under his bedroom window was the
best treasure ever.

A chest filled with his favorite toys.

So he sat down and began to play.